THE NATURAL GUARD

THE NATURAL GUARD

MIKE L. CHAPLA

LitPrime Solutions
485c US Highway 1 South
Suite 100
Iselin, NJ 08830
www.litprime.com
Phone: 1-800-981-9893

Published by LitPrime Solutions: 07/19/2024

ISBN: 979-8-88703-376-1(sc)
ISBN: 979-8-88703-377-8(e)

Library of Congress Control Number: 2024913601

Contents

INTRODUCTION

The late 60's and early 70's were trying, chaotic times. The war in Viet Nam was raging, and those who would end it (the Kennedy brothers) had both been assassinated. Both assassinations are the subject of many books. Suffice it here to say that Lee Harvey Oswald and Sirhan Sirhan were both indced patsics. The military industrial complex (which President Eisenhower had warned of) was dictating policy, making money hand over fist, and causing the slaughter of our best and our most patriotic. College students (myself included) were all trying to obtain and keep our 2S (student) draft status, while others were either heading for Canada or protesting in the streets.

When graduation day finally came, the student deferment went away and the choice had to be made. Wait to be drafted or go to Canada. Neither of these were ultimately appealing. The National Guard was the only option that worked if you were ready to defend your own homeland, but not ready to throw yourself into the middle of a foreign country and a foreign war.

The new National Guard consisted of the old school lifers mixed with recent college graduates which sometimes resembled mixing oil and water. Sometimes, however, this union went surprisingly well.

This book is an indictment of nobody. Everyone who faced the dilemma of making a choice had their own personal reasons for doing what they did. This book is dedicated to those more than 58,000 who made the ultimate sacrifice and to those countless thousands more who came home changed for life, either physically or mentally, or both.

The book is a work of fiction. Any resemblance to actual people, living or dead is coincidental.

CHAPTER 1

The empty glass beer bottle hit the rim of the metal waste basket with a loud CLANK. Thankfully, the basket was half full of old magazines and the bottle bounced from side to side, staying intact and finally nestling into a comfortable spot between Life and Playboy. "Those fucking assholes!" Paul Sanders was officially on a roll. The tirade had begun after Sanders had read a newspaper article about the upcoming draft lottery. Blowers, Kreis, Howard, Longley, Ratterman and I all cringed. The war in Vietnam was not a welcome topic of conversation, especially in a college dormitory.

"Not only are they going to draft us, but they're going to have a lottery based on our birthdays. They're gonna play fucking bingo with our lives!" Sanders had taken a final swig of his beer and had thrown the empty across the room, accidentally making a shot that Dr. J would be proud of. The sound of glass bouncing off metal rang out the open door into the hall. "Jesus Christ, I'm trying to study here!" came a loud reply from somewhere down the hall.

"You can call me JC and I'm fresh out of miracles so your grades will stay in the shitter no matter how hard you study."

"Very funny. Now keep it down, dickhead."

"Anybody else hungry?" I made a heroic attempt to change the subject. For naught.

"Who in the fuck is studying on Saturday night?" Bob Rizucco yelled from the next room to no one in particular.

"It's me, Bill Connolly" came the response from down the hall, aimed at no one in particular.

"I thought your room was on second floor."

"It is. I'm in Cranstead's room. Shaving cream war on my floor. I could eat, though. Anybody there hungry?"

I watched in awe as Jim Blawers carefully selected a 45 rpm record from a huge stack. With amazing dexterity, the black plastic disk was hurled at an angle out of the room and into the hallway where it crashed against the far brick wall, shattering into a million pieces.

"Blawers is still playing records, huh? Cease fire." Connolly abandoned his intellectual pursuits and joined the rest of us in Blowers' room.

"Who's making the food run, Chaps?" Connolly, the captain of the rugby team inquired of me, a winger who he and others had induced to play a sport I knew nothing about.

A sport which had introduced me to some of the finer experiences of life, like urinating blood.

"I'll drive." Said Steve Howard, the saint-like roommate of Jim Blowers. Anyone who could put up with the perversion that was Blowers deserved to be canonized. After what seemed like an eternity of taking orders and collecting money, Howard and Connolly headed out into the night in search of fries, cokes, and chilidogs.

After apologizing to the hall monitor for Blowers' vinyl assault on the wall, I looked around. The prospect of food must have taken Sanders' mind off being blown up in Vietnam. He was nowhere to be seen.

"Hey Paul, where'd you go?"

"I'm in here, weenie." The echo had resounded into the hallway from an open bathroom door. "I'm a little drunk".

"Not really. You must be close to 200 pounds."

"Very funny." The echo got closer as I approached. Turning the corner into the communal bathroom, I observed Sanders seated in a chair in front of one of the urinals.

"You are going to piss all over your pants."

"I kept on peeing on the wall when I was standing up. Then I almost fell down."

"Hopefully you'll be sobered up by the time you have to take a dump."

Assessing the situation, I ascertained that Sanders had successfully emptied his bladder. The telltale wet line down his crotch would dry quickly. I helped him to his feet and we limped back to Blowers' room.

Blowers was the epitome of scam and scum combined. He had successfully conned the world into thinking he was human. He was a successful student, held a good job, and had a sweet, attractive girlfriend. He delighted in playing the role of model student, employee and boyfriend when in public. Those of us who knew him, however, learned early that he was the king of crude and the ghost of gross. Blowers had prepared a surprise for Howard and Connolly when they returned with the food.

He had lowered the elastic waistband of his tighty whiteys to beneath his testicles which resembled two over-inflated balloons as they bulged out of his pants. He lay on his bed in this pose, patiently waiting to see how long it would take everyone to notice. "Very nice",

I commented. "But you should really get those fixed. You could go blind". Blowers knew I was used to his act, but he was still giddy with anticipation. "Are they back yet?"

Just then Howard and Connoly, having made their way up the dorm stairs with the treasured food, came up the hall. Howard turned the corner and entered the room, already digging into the bag of food. "Who had the…YOU SICK FUCK!" As he screamed at Blowers, Howard hurled the first cheeseburger that he had come across at the bed, squarely hitting Blowers in the bulging, exposed onions. As Blowers screamed in pain, the rest of us experienced the same thought. "You're eating that one, asshole!" Longley put it into words for the rest of us, who were busy trying to catch our breath amid hysterical laughter. In spite of his many flaws, Blowers could always take your mind off the war, if only for a few seconds.

After consuming multiple burgers, chili-dogs, and fries, the conversation turned to daily college life, to include teachers, sports, and most-importantly, women.

CHAPTER 2

After the feeding frenzy at the Blowers residence, I made my way out of the dorm into the cold snowy parking lot. I crackled and crunched my way through the crusted snow, finally arriving at the back door of the fieldhouse. Pulling open the door, I basked in the rush of warm, humid air. The hoop heads were water bugging back and forth under the gym baskets, shoes squeaking a sweaty symphony.

It was after 9:00 p.m. so the pool was closed to public swimming. I cracked the combo lock and fished my cold, damp, silky swim trunks out of my locker. As I pulled them on, my nuts shrieked and attempted to hide in my throat. I wondered to myself why I was choosing to repeat this daily ritual on a perfectly good weekend night. I was hardly an indispensable member of the swim team, mainly competing as the freestyle leg of relays.

Purposely leaving the overhead pool lights off, I walked slowly to the edge of the empty pool and gazed at the glistening water and the underwater lights. There was something so hypnotic, surreal and peaceful about swimming in the dark that I had come to need. The friendly world that I had known in my youth had been replaced by a menacing, confusing combination of fear and undesirable choices. My country wanted me to arm myself and take sides in a civil war on the other side of the world – a war that wasn't mine – a war in which the good guys and the bad guys looked the same. I doubted my ability to take another man's life under these or any other circumstances. I was afraid.

Diving in, I let the soothing embrace of the water surround me and take me completely out of the real world. Nothing could hurt me here.

CHAPTER 3

The draft "lottery" came and went. Peoples' lives were validated and destroyed. On campus, it didn't take a rocket scientist to tell who was who. If he was walking like the living dead and his girlfriend beside him was in tears, his birthday had come up early. If he had a little kid's bounce in his step and his grin was reminiscent of a monstrous, shit eating Cheshire cat, his birthday had been selected late enough that his number would not be called. The difference was readily apparent in the classroom. Some attacked their studies with new vigor, knowing that a civilian career would follow their degree. Others lost all motivation, knowing that Uncle Sam would be waiting to swap an M-16 for their diploma.

Some of us straddled the line between the two. My birthday had been selected number 170. I was neither definitively a permanent civilian nor certain fodder for the Viet Cong. This limbo-like existence became intolerable after a couple of months, so I made a call to my local draft board.

"No sir, you won't be drafted" the voice stated with authority, making my heart soar and my feet nearly break into a rhythm-less white boy dance. ... "today" the other shoe dropped. " It may be as long as two weeks before you get your draft notice and come in for your physical exam". Swallowing the "Aw fuck" that immediately appeared on my tongue, I thanked the kind lady and hung the phone up.

I began to experience some of the benefits of having my own mortality shoved down my throat and up my ass simultaneously. First, I began to appreciate the simple things of life – sunshine, laughter, friends. Second, I gradually came to the realization that, no matter how different we are, we all need each other. When the alternative is never hanging out with anyone ever again, it's pretty easy to put aside personal biases and actually enjoy being able to hang out with someone you normally can't stand.

It was the second realization that brought me to Blowers. As was his custom, Blowers had used the draft like he used everything else. He turned it into an opportunity to totally fuck with the minds of those around him. His draft number was 364. He was as safe as a baby tucked in a crib. He enlisted.

CHAPTER 4

Hendrix was coming. In a miraculous turn of events, the legendary lefty would actually perform on our campus. It seemed incongruous that the Jimi Hendrix Experience would be performing in the fieldhouse of a Jesuit college. I wondered how much Hendrix, Mitchell, and Redding knew about Jesuit education. I also wondered how much the Jesuits knew about Hendrix and crew. The event promised to be interesting at the very least.

Having purchased our Hendrix tickets, Ratterman, Longley, Kreis, and I set out on the long, lonely task of obtaining female accompaniment for the concert. The school year was relatively new, so our reputations hadn't yet been irreparably but deservedly soiled. We would impinge upon a classmate to arrange victims (i.e. dates) for us. We would deftly execute a trial run and the girls who survived that test would advance to the concert round of the competition. The Royal Platte River Yacht Club, aka the Grabba Bitta Snatch fraternity was open for business. Our yacht club T shirts had special local significance, as the Platte River was the local sewage dump.

Ergo, our motto was inscribed on the back of our shirts "We're dipped in shit".

Saturday night, better known as date night, was always chaotic in the dorms. People ran hither and yon, looking to borrow after shave or to ask their benefactor a last question about a blind date. The question part always amused me because the guys who always asked the most questions about their prospective dates were generally the guys who should have been happy to date Freddy Krueger's older sister. There was an art to blind dating – the cultivation of an attitude. That attitude was pretty much encapsulated in two words – "Fuck it".

I had stopped by the dorm to visit with Steve Adamle, who actually had a bona fide date that he had actually previously seen. They had been going out for a few weeks and were, as the Turtles put it, "Happy Together". I wanted to be near Adamle before going out just in case some of his mojo might rub off.

As I stepped through the door to his room, I observed a lonely figure holding his head in one hand and a magazine in another. He had been reading about the war in the latest Time magazine and greeted me with "Dear God, please don't let me catch my lunch in Viet Nam." With a quick "Amen", I made my immediate exit. That kind of mojo I already had.

I made my way out of the dorm and into the parking lot, jumped into my 1962 Austin Healey 3000, and headed for Longley's house. The Healey was bright red and had cost me $1,000. It had a few idiosyncrasies like a removable gear shift. Not the gear shift nob. The entire gear shift could be lifted out of the transmission whenever I so chose. I usually removed it and used it to wave at people.

CHAPTER 5

Tonight the crew was headed for a mixer at a local girls' college. Hopefully, one or more of us would actually get a female to dance without her losing a bet. Kreis, Longley, and I rode together in Kreis's Chevy Corvair. I wasn't overly enthused about any car that had no engine in the front. Lack of an engine did have one advantage that we used on occasion. Longley had procured a three foot long plastic spark plug. No one knew where he had gotten it. No one asked. It was too much fun just using it. This night we first headed to 16th St., the main drag in the downtown area. It was also the designated cruising and car show area.

There was no shortage of exhibitionists displaying custom cars and custom women as we turned onto the one way street. The Corvair took its place proudly in the midst of Mustangs, Vettes, and Camaros. We got more than one look from drivers whose expressions said "What the fuck are you guys doing here?" Then, Kreis deftly put the plan into action. He alternately hit the brake and gas pedals as if the car was choking down its last gallon of gas in gulps. After about a block of feigned automotive duress, Kreis brought the courageous Corvair to an abrupt halt. Immediately, the angry chorus of car horns began as Longley exited the car and headed for the front of the car. Of course, there was no engine in the front of the car, just a trunk containing a three foot long plastic spark plug. Kreis popped the latch to the trunk and Longley lifted the trunk lid and scratched his head, as if pondering a problem.

He reached under the open lid and pulled the huge plastic sparkplug out into the night air. The chorus of our laughter was only drown out by the chorus of everyone else's "what the fuck is that?" Deftly, he righted the fake sparkplug and began twisting it, as if to screw it back in where it belonged.

By now, we had created enough of a commotion to attract the attention of the local police, who were charged with keeping order during the festivities. As an officer of the law approached, he caught a glimpse of Longley's plastic spark plug and not so silently said "what the fuck?" Our pending arrest, a jail cell, and visions of sugar plum fairies named Rocco danced through my head. Then, as if by divine intervention, a leggy blonde caught the attention of the policeman (and everyone else's). Not only did she catch his attention, but she planted a big smackeroo right on his kisser. "She must like cops", I muttered, right before I said "let's get the hell out of here".

Phase 1 of the evening had been completed and we moved along to Phase 2.

CHAPTER 6

Phase 2 of the evening consisted of stopping at one of our favorite watering holes, not so much to water down as to see who might be there that we knew. Also, we had time to burn prior to Phase 3.

As we entered, we were greeted by the sounds of Jimi – "There must be some kind of way out of here." "Jimi is spending entirely too much time along the Watchtower" Longley offered. "It's just not healthy." "Thanks for that astute observation" Kreis responded, "you should really talk to him when he gets here." "Good point."

Entering the bar, I heard a laugh that I knew but couldn't place. I knew that I hadn't heard it in a long while and that intrigued me. As we moved through the crowded tavern, I heard that familiar voice again, this time calling my name. "Hey Mikey, over here." I looked over to see a blast from the past – Steve Massuga, from the old neighborhood. "Hey buddy", I called out as I made my way over to him. I soon was stopped in my tracks. Something wasn't right. He was in a wheelchair. His legs were missing.

Immediately my thoughts flashed back to our childhood. Steve was not only an exceptional athlete, but also narrated the games that he was playing in. In baseball, he could hit the ball a mile and would follow up his crushing swing with "that ball was tagged…" as he rounded the bases. I loved and admired the guy.

I had heard that Steve had done a tour in Viet Nam, but had no idea that he was back. I tried to avert my gaze from his missing legs, but he began talking. " Mikey, tell me that you are in school and that you will stay in school. I nodded in the affirmative. " If you don't, I will track you down and whip your skinny ass." "I would go back if I could".. he continued "but you need to stay away from that fucking place".

I kissed him on top of the head and tried to stay out of his line of sight as tears began to well up in my eyes. I managed to choke out a "great to see you, brother. I love you."

I knew he had seen the tears when he replied "I love you too, you little weasel. Now get the fuck out of here."

"You guys ready to roll out? The numbness of seeing one of my neighborhood favorites devastated by a fucked up war was starting to wear off. It was starting to hurt. I needed to get out of the bar – now.

CHAPTER 7

Phase 3 of the evening's festivities consisted of our attendance at that most notorious of all college activities, "the mixer". Local girls' schools usually sponsored at least one per year. By the beginning of the following year, the memories of last year's mixcr had thankfully dwindlcd.

Arriving at our destination in Kreis's magnificent machine, we parked where no one could see us and made the trek into the gymnasium to join the rest of the restless revelers. By now over half of the attendees from our school were at least half in the bag. It seems that the prospect of meeting an actual female was just too much for some.

We made an inconspicuous entrance and headed for a corner from which to observe the goings on. Almost as soon as we had arrived at our vantage point, an attractive co-ed approached and announced "Hi, my name is Sarah." My first thoughts were "Hi, Sarah, what the fuck is wrong with you? Do you have a disease? Death wish? Wooden leg? I know – you must be blind." Instead, I responded.

"Hi, I'm Michael. At your cervix." My timing was off a bit as Sarah was taking a sip of her Coke at the time of my greeting and she shot some from her mouth and some from her nose. "You asshole!" she said politely, as I grabbed some napkins and helped her clean up. "Payback is a bitch." She responded. "Just remember that." Thus was the beginning of a beautiful relationship.

How come girls can always dance and guys can't? Sarah and I called a truce long enough to hit the dance floor and at one point, she said "Jesus, dude, you really are a white guy." After thanking her for her astute observation, I decided to get really white. I spun around, twirling awkwardly and did a three stooges move by putting my hand on the floor and running in circles. Sarah decided not to join the thunderous applause. "Let's go sit down, Curley Joe," she said, "before you hurt yourself.

The lights were eventually turned on, announcing the end of the evening. Just then, one of our illustrious classmates vomited at the exit door. Sanders, who had been following much too closely, slid clumsily in the nasty stuff, but managed not to fall. Unfortunately, a girl who was also in the area saw Paul slide and heaved her approval, blowing massive amounts of chunks all over. And another college memory is chalked up.

CHAPTER 8

was fairly sure that I could talk Sarah into going to the Hendrix concert with me, although the ticket price was a bit exorbitant - $3 apiece. I was right. She was psyched to see Jimi, Mitch, and Noel – the entire Jimi Hendrix Experience. Since I had purchased the tickets prior to asking her, I was relieved that I wouldn't have to wear an "I'm Stagg" sign all night.

The concert was in the field house, which meant that the locker room that the swim team occupied would have to be altered "somewhat". "Somewhat" consisted of a complete overhaul complete with dim, red lighting. Swim practice was cancelled for the day which was fine with me since I had no desire to get in touch with the part of me which longed to become someone associated with red lights.

Steve Howard was part of a team of students charged with getting the band situated and taken care of. He caught up with the rest of us in the student center. He had a Cheshire cat type grin on his face when we saw him. "What's so funny?" I asked.

"We were setting up the dressing room and Hendrix brought in his guitar case. I thought that I would get a close-up glimpse of the Hendrix axe."

"And...." I inquired. "Instead of his guitar, he had bottles of vodka, bourbon, scotch, and rum tucked neatly into his guitar case."

"Sweet..." I replied.

The concert was awesome. Hendrix and company were great. Unfortunately, the opening band – not so much. First off, the drummer came out shirtless which might have worked at another venue, but not this one. One of the Jesuit fathers made it quite clear that no shirt, no play. After the drummer donned his shirt, most of the concert goers started to regret the choice the drummer had made. The lead singer launched into a monotonous chorus of "I did it again, I did it again, I did it again, and then I did it again...ad infinitum, ad nauseam. He must have gone on like this for twenty minutes. Finally the crowd decided that it had enough and began to boo and throw things. The band finally caught on and brought the band's whatever it was to a close.

If some of the concert goers were ambivalent toward the Hendrix experience, the opening act cured that. Jimi and the boys were greeted to a thunderous welcome. They began with "Purple Haze" with Jimi throwing in a little twist - instead of singing "'scuse me, while I kiss the sky, he sang "'scuse me, while I kiss this guy" and gave his drummer, Mitch Mitchell a kiss on the head.

After the concert, which Sarah loved, she began a lecture as to why Hendrix and other musicians participated in pyrotechnics, and the destruction of their instruments. Something about trying and being unable to reach perfection in their music.

CHAPTER 9

Like all good things, the college experience comes and goes in a flash. Soon, the crew had accepted their diplomas and had gone our separate ways. The last person that I saw was Blowers, with whom I spent the day of my pre-induction physical. It was a fairly standard physical, with the obligatory pants drop and head turn while an ex-con pretending to be a doctor made sure that everyone's testicles were securely fastened and weren't going to escape out of anyone's pantleg. The highlight of the day was when one of the recruits misheard the doc say "turn your head and cough". He thought that the doc had said "turn your hand and cough." The recruit obediently began gyrating his wrist like it was on a ball bearing. Needless to say, this perturbed the doc greatly, as did the laughter coming from the rest of us.

With the physical behind me, there was now nothing to stop me from joining my National Guard unit and becoming a savage, barbaric, Attilla the Hun type character. As I prepared to attend my unit's first meeting, I practiced snorting, spitting, and cursing so I would be sure to fit in.

The first meeting of my National Guard unit was fittingly on a gloomy day in which the clouds hung suspended and at times actually touched the ground. As I turned onto the base, I noticed that there were other recruits dressed in civilian clothes. I wasn't alone. Hooray.

The barracks were vintage WWII, mostly made of wood. I pulled my car next to an old Bronco II on the dirt in the non-existent parking lot. Getting out of my car, I caught the pungent scent of marijuana. Looking around, I saw that I wasn't the only recruit that had caught a whiff of cannabis. Others were looking around while walking toward the barracks and chuckling to themselves.

Suddenly, a soldier with his uniform in shreds came running toward us. He was followed by a number of fully dressed soldiers who were apparently intent on ripping his clothes off. With his shirt and pants in tatters and his boxer shorts in full view, he made it to his car with a huge grin on his face. It was his last official meeting. I silently wondered if they would let me leave if I ripped my clothing off. Nah.

Filing into the ancient building which was to be the site of our meetings, I noticed that there were a number of other recruits who didn't have uniforms. Apparently, only after going to basic training were we allowed to look official.

Examining the interior of the wooden barracks, I discovered that the bathroom actually had three stalls where the shitters were. Unfortunately, the stalls were doorless, so that, if you were stinking up the joint, you were looking directly at the person who was the beneficiary of your smelly efforts.

Making the rounds, I discovered that some folks, uniformed or not, had coffee.

There appeared to be a problem, though. There seemed to be an awful lot of complaints about said coffee. The complaints were quickly addressed by the cook who enlightened everyone by stating, "You guys didn't complain about the coffee last month and it's the same coffee. I just reheated it." I passed on the coffee.

Then it was time for the official formation and roll call. We newbies scrambled to make sure that we were either standing behind someone in uniform or another newbie. Those who were standing behind a uniform soon learned formation lesson #1 – be careful who you get behind. There were several gassy discharges from the front rows, followed by snorts and giggling. As names were called and answered to, some were accompanied by a half choking and half groaning sound. I could hardly believe how glamourous Army life was.

Our company was part of a signal battalion and was now made up of new recruits who were almost all college graduates and the full time National Guardsmen who made it a career. For the most part, things went better than I had expected as most of the unit showed respect for each other. Some of the "lifers" even helped us new guys prepare for basic training by telling us what to expect and teaching us marching techniques like turns, about face, etc. We spent most pre-basic meetings marching, talking sports, and eating.

When the word came down about our basic training, we were somewhat less than stoked.

We would be going to Fort Jackson, South Carolina at the end of June. Three months in a sauna – sweet!

CHAPTER 10

After arriving in Columbia, S.C. via Atlanta, Ga., we arrived by bus at the gates of Fort Jackson at around midnight. An unnecessarily gleeful individual greeted us with "Y'all probably ain't gonna like Fort Jackson, but it's gonna love you!" Thanks for the pep talk, bruh.

Departing the bus at the reception station, we prepared ourselves for some type of sleep, however brief. Instead, we were hustled to the mess hall and served a midnight snack of red beans and rice. Welcome to the South, boys. Admittedly, the meal was very tasty and hit the spot. The first impression of the food was a good one and subsequent meals didn't change that. Army food was surprisingly good.

The Colorado boys were separated into different companies, along with the boys from Alabama and the boys from Louisiana. We would see each other in passing and would inquire of each other regarding important matters. The question of the day was "did you poop yet?" Any type of affirmation was greeted with great glee and high fives.

One thing that the Colorado boys were not prepared for was the language difference. The southern drill instructors spoke so rapidly and so "southern" that we couldn't make heads or tails out of what they were saying. It was usually something important that they expected us to do. Our only recourse was to find another soldier who was from the South and do whatever he was doing. Needless to say, the drill instructors were not pleased with our looks of befuddlement or our failure to immediately "snap to" whatever directive they gave. It became a game of "Simon sez let's see how long it takes you fucking Colorado tardos to figure out what is going on and what we expect you to do."

June is not a good month to ship from the reception station to the basic training barracks. At least not when you're in South Carolina. Temperature 110 degrees, 96 percent humidity. If you are from Colorado, you look and smell like a wet dog.

In their infinite mercy, the drill instructors took us to the mess hall and gave us a dixie cup of kool aid and some sugar cookies. Everyone drank their kool aid in an instant, left their sugar cookies, and anticipated a refill on the kool aid. Negative. Back out to the barracks for cleaning duty.

One of the instructional classes of basic was the assembly and disassembly of the M-16 rifle, followed by daily treks up "drag ass hill" to the range. Most of us found this a reasonably beneficial experience as we enjoyed target practice at home and the M-16 was fun to shoot. The fun ended when one of the drill instructors, fresh from Viet Nam, demonstrated the use of a bayonette. There aren't many harmless scenarios that you can think of when someone is shoving a knife, which is at the end of a rifle, into what may have once been a punching bag.

There was quite a bit of extracurricular duty to keep one busy outside of training – KP duty, Fireguard duty, CQ runner, etc. You might get lucky and get KP duty during the daytime, but fireguard and CQ runner were at night when everyone was sleeping. This would generally render you useless for training the next day.

Naturally, I had fireguard duty the night before we had to throw live grenades. Sweet. The course was set up with a number of stations, each with a concrete wall about five yards out. Inside, there was a funnel into a reinforced hole in case a grenade was dropped and needed to be kicked into a place that was non-lethal to the participants. The participants consisted of a trainee and an instructor. What could go wrong?

Everything. I was handed my first grenade, gripped it in my left (throwing) hand and grasped the pin with my right hand. Unfortunately, my right hand was sweaty and came off the pin when I tried to pull it. Shit. The instructor shouted "stop", my brain shouted back "fuck no" and I pulled the pin and threw the grenade with the instructor draped over me like a defensive tackle. The grenade cleared the wall and exploded as the instructor pushed me to the ground and covered me with his body. This struck me as either very heroic or very forward. I didn't even know his name.

I repeated the drill with a second grenade and had no problems. The damage, however, had been done. I was now dubbed a fuckup who needed extra attention. Great. Actually, when I really think about it, my parents always knew that I was a fuckup who needed extra attention. If it looks like a duck, and fucks up like a duck, it's probably a duck.

Meanwhile, while I was finding new ways to fuck up, there were those who had this Army shit down. And they were punished appropriately. David Centry, for example. He shot a perfect score in qualification and didn't have to walk back to quarters. A car picked him up and drove him back. When the rest of us got back, we expected to see him lounging and drinking a Coke. Instead, he was busy cleaning every weapon in the company. Maybe being a fuckup isn't so bad.

CHAPTER 11

Not having anything to lose is a feeling of complete freedom. Freedom to take a stand for fuckups everywhere. For example, kitchen police duty seems fairly innocuous. Approached with the correct attitude, however, it can become an opportunity to mess with folks in the mess hall.

I was in the serving line next to a fellow grunt named Kowalski. Being partly of Polish descent myself, I took the opportunity to exercise my God-given right to correct a long-standing injustice. I was in charge of serving the French toast, but could think of no good reason for calling it French toast. So, if you wanted some of this particular dish, you had to call it by its new designation – Polish toast.

My first few patrons asked for my dish by its former name, French toast. I informed them that we had nothing by that name. When they pointed and asked "what is that, then?" I informed them that this delicacy was now known as Polish toast. A hungry soldier will do anything for food and soon I had the entire mess hall asking for

Polish toast. A small step for man, a giant step for Polish people everywhere.

Having done my civic duty for the day, it was time for inoculations. We were lined up like good cattle and rolled up both our sleeves, walking until we were between two medics, each of whom had an air gun which injected whatever it was into our arms. Of course, the operation was preceded by the obligatory horror story of the trainee who moved as the shot was administered and who suffered a torn and bleeding arm. Having been at KP duty for the day, there was more of a chance that I would fall asleep than that I would move my arm.

My final gig of basic training (the night before we left) was CQ runner. The base has a nightly person who is in Charge of Quarters who had one or two "runners" to do any errands that the CQ wanted done. I had drawn a CQ named White who had a reputation as a real ball buster. By this time, I was so giddy with the thought of leaving basic that nothing could phase me now. I even showed up early for my CQ runner gig. The guy who was on duty with me was apparently not so optimistic. He showed up late and got a real earful. Meanwhile, Sgt. White used me as an example of a good soldier who met his duties head on and on time. He was simultaneously raking my co-runner over the coals and began thinking up trivia for him to do.

As the evening went along, Sgt. White and I spoke about our philosophies and life in general. White's family had a mortuary business in Atlanta, which he would be taking over upon his discharge from the army. He confided that he had wickedly earned his reputation and needed to right things with the Good Lord. I told him that the Lord was quick to forgive and, if he took care of the families who were grieving at the mortuary, he would be doing the Lord's work and would be rewarded accordingly.

CHAPTER 12

The two weeks after basic training were gone in two seconds, although Sarah and I made the most of those two seconds. We were both in love and did not hesitate to demonstrate that whenever and wherever we could – my room, her room, my car, her car, in public, etc. You get the picture.

Now it was time for AIT (Advanced Individual Training). Since we were a Signal unit, our AIT was conducted at Fort Gordon, Georgia. Fort Gordon was an amazing change from Fort Jackson. We were housed in buildings, not barracks, and treated like real soldiers, not grunts. To be fair, Fort Jackson pretty much had to treat us like grunts, because we were. Lastly, and most importantly, the food was good, just like at Jackson.

When I got situated in my new home, I took inventory of those I would share my living quarters with. There was my bud from home Don Calibrese, whom I was psyched to have with me and on whom I knew I could rely. There was Bobby Goble from Pittsburgh, who was very young and thus appropriately crazy. Every good team has to have a cowboy and we were no different. Derry Pasternak was our cowboy, complete with rodeo experience and the belt buckles to match. Richard C. Thomas was an amazing guitar player who would put us to sleep by playing "If I Fell" by the Beatles. Last, but far from least was Robert Romero whose music of choice (only music of choice) came from a group called Little Joe and the Latineers. Robert and I did not share musical tastes, but were both fans of Notre Dame football, so all was good.

Our workday started at 3p.m. and lasted til midnight. We were training on old signal equipment although the Army had much newer stuff. We trained on the equipment that we would have when we got back to Colorado. One of us would be charged with getting the platoon to and from class. Lots of freedom. The instructors were very good.

As time went by, we got to know all of the idiosyncrasies each other had. These were all trumped by the young-un, Bobby Goble. He had this weird habit of squirting lighter fluid into his mouth, lighting his lighter, and spitting the lighter fluid out into a huge ball of flame. The rest of us neither dared nor cared to compete with that. Go figure.

The highlight of each day was mail call for a couple of reasons. Obviously, if you got mail, that made your day. Also, there was one soldier whose name was Ducket. If he got mail, the entire formation broke out in song: "Rubber Ducket, you're the one". When you're in the Army, you find your entertainment wherever and whenever you can.

There was one day, however, that didn't go as well for me. I did get mail from home, but the news wasn't good – first, my cousin's husband had come home from work to find her lifeless body – she was in her 20's. Nobody knew what exactly had happened. Next, a friend of mine with whom I had gone to grade school, had been killed in Viet Nam.

There was no escaping life's realities – not even in the Army. Classes followed mail call, so I didn't have time to ponder these events or feel sorry for myself. That was a good thing.

Apparently, my demeanor was sufficient to indicate that something was wrong, so Goble decided to lighten (really lighten) the mood by doing his fire spewing when the CQ runner went room to room indicating lights out.

As soon as Pasternak switched the lights off, Goble unleashed a ball of fire that would have made a fire breathing dragon proud. It was quite a dramatic show. The CQ runner was less than pleased, but did not suffer any injuries as Goble had been situated well away from the door. Another day in Paradise.

AIT was going amazingly well. It's crazy how good it feels to be treated like a legitimate human being.

Unfortunately, there was one more exercise that had to be conquered before AIT came to a close. We had to pull an outdoor, overnight training session which consisted of breaking down and moving an existing communications center and re-establishing the lines of communication.

This maneuver might have been challenging if the overnight weather was decent. Unfortunately, the gorgeous Georgia weather decided not to cooperate. There have been many comparisons to cold weather – a witch's tit, a golddigger's ass in Alaska, etc. However, none of these hold a candle to 14 degrees in Augusta, Georgia. In Colorado, you can put on several layers of clothing and be fairly comfortable. In Georgia, the humidity will watch you try to insulate yourself while it laughs hysterically. The fucking water trailer froze solid.

Apparently, we had already embarked on our ill-fated journey when the company commander was informed that 14 degrees was well under the temperature in which all troops must be removed from the field. He later explained that we were already out there, and that we would be better off staying in the field and completing the mission rather than doing it all again.

As the night progressed, we moved from station to station in the back of an open deuce and a half. I later thought that this would be a perfect solution to all race problems, because we all piled into the back of the deuce and a half, not caring at all who we were lying on top of or under. Mother Nature doesn't fuck around with such petty things as racism. When you are freezing your ass, all mankind are your brothers.

CHAPTER 13

Having completed the freeze fest, it was time to say bye-bye to Fort Gordon and AIT. I would reunite with some of my brothers back in Colorado, but I knew that I would never see some of my roomies and friends ever again. Some had orders for Viet Nam. That really sucked.

Making the rounds, I advised Goble to find a different way to amuse himself that didn't involve massive fireballs. Just said goodbye to Pasternak because I knew that telling him to give up broken bones and rodeo would never fly. I advised Thomas that I would probably never get to sleep again without hearing his rendition of "If I Fell". Romero and I made a pledge to toast every touchdown that the Irish scored in their upcoming bowl game.

As we exited the gates of Fort Gordon, we were behind another member of our guard unit, Don Foley. As soon as his sports car left Fort Gordon behind, Don left his army uniform behind also. Throwing pants, shirts, skivvies, socks, etc. on the road, he left us to wonder if he was going to drive back to Colorado naked. Luckily, we never got close enough to find out.

CHAPTER 14

Having completed basic training and A.I.T., It was time to get into a normal routine again. This included National Guard meetings once a month. Now that we were grizzled veterans, we dressed for meetings like the rest of the troops. For whatever reason, I kind of liked the idea of everyone looking the same it had an equalizing effect on us.

The "new guys" definitely added a different way of looking at things. When we trained with riot batons, it was hard to think of an enemy who looked like a college student. We had all just recently left the college scene and we had no animosity for those who would demonstrate against the war in Viet Nam. So, we added our own special sauce to our riot training. The powers that be made the mistake of putting myself and Ron Hurtado in charge of a riot baton training exercise, so, when all of the authorities had left us to our own devices, we demonstrated a method of calming the rioters, instead of bashing them. We did our own rendition of the song "Me and my Shadow" using riot batons as props in the place of the canes that Danny Kay and Fred Astaire would have used. I hate to brag, but we got a standing ovation from the troops (still counts even if there was no place to sit).

We actually did get called up when a local college had students camping on school grounds, calling themselves "Woodstock West". We met at the base one afternoon and the plan was to show up and disperse the students early the next morning. Fortunately, one of our troops stopped by the makeshift village on his way home and advised them of the situation. The next morning, only one lonely straggler was left and one of our guys patted him on the butt and sent him on his way. Mission accomplished.

Sports was always a big deal, whether we were talking about a recent heavyweight fight or tossing around a football after lunch or during a break. If we couldn't scrounge up a football, a softball or even a wiffle ball would work. Army boots weren't the lightest footwear, but, as long as everyone was sporting them, games were always competitive.

CHAPTER 15

Having become a real national guardsman, I wondered how Sarah would feel about the fact that I was now committed to one weekend a month and two weeks in the summer. She totally surprised me with a suggestion that we get our own apartment. She was gainfully employed at a local hospital, while I worked at a local bank. Monthly rent was not a problem, and we enjoyed sharing our new living quarters. We may have enjoyed them a little too much, as she soon became pregnant. This was a joy to both of us and really cemented our commitment to each other. To put it mildly, I was happy as a hog in slop.

As summer approached, so did the two week commitment known as summer camp. Summer camp consisted of a convoy of deuce and a half trucks carrying radio equipment into the mountains of the great (dismally barren) state of Wyoming. We would set up radio antennas and establish a network of communications, which we would then break down and move to another locale. On the weekend, we would all be left to our own devices, to rest, explore etc. A good time would be had by all.

On the morning that we were to leave for summer camp, roll call came up one man short. Specialist Fourth Class Revers was nowhere to be found. Since one monkey don't stop no show, preparations to leave were begun anyway. As prep was concluded, lo and behold, who shows up but Revers. As it turns out, he has just had time to grab his gear after being released from jail. Demon Rum had claimed another victim as Revers did not fail his field sobriety test, he fell down trying to get his wallet out of his pants. This is what is referred to in law enforcement as a "clue".

As the caravan of Army trucks made its way up the highway, I soon discovered why we were going well below the speed limit. As the truck approached 60 mph, the steering wheel would shake so violently that it was incredibly hard to slow down fast enough to stop the shaking. This was quite unnerving for both the driver and passenger. Needless to say, one of these episodes was enough to guarantee that, henceforth, the vehicle speed would hover around the 50 mph mark.

Summer camp would be conducted in the mountains above a small Wyoming town. As we drove through the town, I noticed a huge cardboard cutout in front of the town's only bar. The cutout depicted a beaten down soldier being lassoed by a smiling cowboy. Ah, those Wyoming folk sure know how to make a bunch of guys feel welcome.

As we arrived at our mountain destination, each of us partnered with another "camper" and assembled our pup tent with two shelter halves.

Each of us had a sleeping bag with an accompanying blow-up air mattress. All but one had a corresponding rubber cork which kept the air mattress from leaking air.

As it so happens, when I buy lottery tickets, I rarely match one number, much less win anything. When faced with one in one hundred odds of getting the one air mattress without a cork, I totally obliterated those fucking odds. Likewise, I destroyed the odds of my bunkmate being a non-snorer. Bob Young's snoring was a combination of a cat fight and a buzz saw.

I immediately set about trying to find any piece of wood that I could stuff into the air mattress which would give me time to fall asleep before Young did. Unfortunately, when you are desperately trying to fall asleep quickly, your brain goes a million places, none of which are conducive to relaxation, much less sleep. Ah, the Army life.

One of our first exercises was to break down camp and move to another location while being strafed from above. The caravan was to avoid total demolition by having its trucks alternately move to opposite sides of the road. Simple enough. Simple enough until it isn't.

One element of the drill that wasn't mentioned to the participants was the fact that we would be strafed by an actual plane, being piloted by an individual who was fresh from the Viet Nam war and whose only speed was balls to the wall. As the trucks made their way down the road and took their alternating positions, one of our drivers, who was not known for his discretion, decided to flip the bird at the low flying aircraft. Bad move, very bad move.

The road that our trucks were on was adjacent to a fairly deep ravine. As the pilot disappeared on one horizon, several drivers expressed their dismay with the bird flipper. Meanwhile the pilot (bird flippee) had circled back to make another run. George Konkel was the first to notice. As he looked behind the convoy to the ravine, he managed to spit out three words, "oh, fuck, no".

Our pilot from the not so friendly skies had apparently seen the dipshit who flipped the bird and was none too happy about it. He tucked his plane in the ravine and made his pass at our eye level. On the bright side, we got to see the pilot and his plane up close and personal. On the not so bright side, the sound was so deafening, anyone outside did two things – covered their ears (which didn't help) and dropped to their knees in pain. Needless to say, there was a rush to get to the bird flipper, and he was thoroughly thrashed. Air Force 1, National Guard 0.

CHAPTER 16

One of the high points of summer camp was sports tournaments between companies. The sport that was the main focus of athletic competition was softball, because it could be played with or without a glove for fielding. We were fairly stacked with ringers, as several players, like Bill Wofford and Ron Hurtado, had semi-pro experience. Also, there were those who were just physically gifted, like Andre Washington. Washington was pretty much sculpted out of rock and if he made any type of incidental contact with the ball, it resulted in a long foul ball or a trip around the bases.

The field (using the agricultural definition) was strewn with weeds, gopher holes, and other various hazards. There was a fence that circled the outer perimeter of the outfield which was in poor condition and a real threat to either trip you, or hang you, depending on which part of the fence you were trying to negotiate. Luckily, our best outfielder was Warren Jacks. Jacks, unlike myself, had unlimited confidence. He could play any sport, drive any vehicle, accomplish any task, and do so with a big smile on his face. He not only exuded confidence, but could back up his words in almost all cases. In this particular case, he could go over or under the fence to make a play and catch a fly ball.

This created a controversy as to whether or not a ball which was caught after going over the fence was a home run or a long out. Fortunately, our games were not close enough for this to matter. We swept our games by eight to ten runs each. Jacks took turns negotiating long fly balls by either stopping short of the fence to catching the ball or by going over the fence. He was having fun determining which side of the fence he would place himself. We swept through the competition like a hot knife through butter. Easy as taking candy from a baby (this analogy is valid until you actually try to take candy from a baby).

After softball and a few trips to the beer tent, it was time to attempt to get some sleep. By this time, I had resigned myself to the fact that I would never be able to fall asleep before Young began his nightly snore-fest. I became a ground sleeper. Tonight, it was all good because at midnight I had fire guard duty anyway.

After sending away the previous fire guard a number of times, I decided to leave snore city and go on my rounds as fire guard. As luck would have it, the first generator that I shined my flashlight on was spewing some kind of fluid. I sought out the mechanic who was on duty and he reluctantly abandoned his air mattress (that actually held air) and took a gander at the wounded generator. He went back for his tools and made a quick and painless repair.

The next day, as the company commander made his rounds, he stopped by and gave me an "atta boy, well done". Luckily, it was in front of Hurtado and Wofford, so I could demonstrate my "dats right, I'm bad". They pretended not to be impressed.

CHAPTER 17

With the assistance of a nightly beer tent, things were moving along pretty well with a few minor exceptions. One of these was directly tied to said beer tent and the accompanying hangovers. One morning, when the bleary-eyed troops were assembled, the first sergeant announced that a few lucky troops were headed directly to a rendezvous with the dreaded M60 machine gun. Sans hangover, this would have been a fun gig. With one, however, not so much. The selectees immediately acknowledged their cursed fate with a chorus of groans. Not being among them, I said a silent "thank you" prayer and began my day.

The next glitch came about when our liaison with the Green Berets made somewhat of a mistake when they were complaining of having to eat whatever they could scrounge up, including snails. He immediately chimed in "Escargot! You lucky bastards! All we had last night was steak and beer!

He was immediately removed from his liaison duties.

A little more than half way through camp, Ronnie Hurtado

came to me and said that the First Sergeant wanted to see me. At first, I thought he was kidding, but his demeanor convinced me that he was not.

Reporting to the First Shirt, I was instructed to pack my gear and informed that there was an emergency at home. Sarah had gone into premature labor and needed me there. I packed my stuff as quickly as I could and reported, along with two others, to our designated driver. We would be going back, thankfully, in a regular automobile and not a deuce and a half truck.

CHAPTER 18

Time flies when you're having fun. Time drags when you're going somewhere you should have been yesterday. After we arrived back at base, I shoved my gear into my car and took off for the hospital. I knew that, at 25 weeks, the baby still had a lot of developing to do. I parked just outside the Emergency Room and walked through to the front desk. Inquiring as to the status of Sarah Stewart, I was told that she was in the maternity ward on the fourth floor. I began to get light headed as I made my way to the elevators. An empty stomach plus a traumatic event equals a trip to queer street, as boxers refer to it.

When I arrived at the fourth floor, I was told that Sarah had gone into premature labor, and had delivered a two pound baby boy. Entering her room, I found her with plenty of drugs aboard and fast asleep.

With my mind racing through several hundred scenarios, I was finally able to determine that the baby was in the NICU or Neonatal Intensive Care Unit. The NICU was on the third floor. As I made my way to the elevator, faces became eerily out of shape and disfigured. I was losing it. I tried to stay upright as I got on the elevator and finally reached the third floor.

Several preemies were on the other side of the glass. Most had tubes hooked to them. A number of them had bandages on their heels, as apparently that was where their blood was drawn from. I was really beginning to fade now.

I inquired of a nurse as to my son's status and she went to summon a doctor. Having not recovered from my trip to queer street, I knew that one more shot of bad news would end me. The doctor delivered the final blow: "he didn't make it."

It was a simultaneous head shot and body blow. I lost my balance and fell onto one knee. I made my way to my feet as the doctor turned to leave and muttered something like "sorry".

I don't know how I made it out of the building, but I did. I do remember that tears blurred my vision and I bumped into a few people on my way out. Walking out into the night air, I leaned against the building, slumped into a fetal position, and wept.

CHAPTER 19

People (especially on crime shows) show the victim's family seeking some type of resolution or closure (like finding the victim's body) as if that would make everything better. That (for lack of a better word) is horse shit. When you lose someone close to you, there is no closure. The passage of time makes it easier to function with the gaping hole in your being, but absolutely nothing can fill that hole. You just go about your business as an incomplete being. Sometimes, when you are busy, you forget that the hole is there. It is always there, however, waiting to remind you of your loss. Such is life.

As time passed and I sank back into my routine of work and National Guard meetings, Sarah and I grew apart. We did attend some counseling sessions to no avail. The counselors basically praised both of us for getting through our trials, but said that the chances of happily getting back together after losing a child were slim. Thanks for the encouragement, motherfuckers! I guess losing a child is close to an insurmountable challenge.

As I immersed myself into work and Guard meetings, I went through a "poor you" phase. Everyone wanted to help in some way, but nobody seemed to understand that this was a solo act. I quickly got fed up with the "so sorry's" and found temporary solace in liquor. Thankfully, as liquor goes, I'm pretty much a lightweight. That saved lots of wear and tear on my body and also on my wallet. A few puke-o-ramas convinced me to look elsewhere for relief. I decided to take up a healthier addiction.

One day while walking through the mall, I popped into a bookstore and noticed that they were really pushing "The Complete Book of Running" by Jim Fixx. The mall was also advertising a five mile race which would take place in about a month. I figured that I would be able to choke and puke my way through five miles if I had a month to train. I bought some shoes and began my running career that evening. My first effort ended in approximately one mile with a lot of gasping and a heavy heart. Thankfully, the book really inspired me and, on race day, I joined my fellow runners on my running debut.

As I approached race time, a few things came up that had not yet occurred to me: where and when do I pee? Do I have to carry my car keys during the race if I want to keep it locked? Where in the pack do I fit in?

The last question was the easiest to answer. If nobody is behind you, nobody will see you puking and/or peeing yourself. Or worse. With that in mind, I made my way to the back of the pack. There I found the answers to the other question that I had. Apparently, I had to relieve myself at the port-o-potties that were situated around the starting line. They expected me to "tene aquam" until I reached the finish line. There was no good solution to the key problem: some carried their keys, others had them on a chain around their neck.

I admitted to my fellow runners that this was my first race

competition. They were very encouraging until one of them told me to get some running shoes. I thought I had running shoes. Apparently, I was wearing "tennis shoes" that were made exclusively for tennis. Who knew?

The race began and when the entire mob had passed me, I gave a "gottem right where I want em" yell and started running. I was careful to start slowly as my goal was to finish the race. Period. Then something weird happened. I started to pass people. Young ones, old ones, ones that looked like they could be in the Olympics. I passed a bunch of them. I was nowhere near the leaders, but I wasn't near the tail enders anymore, either. I finished with a time of 45:12 in about 130th place. I would definitely take it.

Nine minute miles wouldn't qualify me for the Olympics, but, in my world, it was a good start. Maybe it was some kind of Guiness record for running five miles in shoes made for tennis. Anyway, I went home tired and happy.

At my next guard meeting, I sought out fellow guardsmen who were also fellow runners. There were a few newbies like myself, and a few hard core runners who were serious. They were all very encouraging and inquiring, asking questions like "what kind of running shoes do you have?" Not wanting to answer "ones that are for tennis", I told them that I hadn't found a shoe that I really liked and asked them about their shoe preference. Got some good tips and never had to discuss my "tenny runners".

After the shoe discussion, we were trucked off base for some "training". Arriving at a shack in the boonies, one had a sense of apprehension because the lieutenants were all very silent. I was about to say that I smelled something fishy when I actually did smell the lovely fragrance of CS gas. As we were herded off the trucks into formation, gas masks were handed out and we were lined up outside the shack. We were ushered into the shack in groups of eight. Upon entering, we were told to acknowledge that the masks worked very well. We all agreed. Once that was made clear, it was time to find out what the masks were protecting us from. On the count of three (for those who didn't cheat) and five for the rest of us, the masks were removed, we blurted out our name, rank, and serial number and then did two laps of the inside of the shack before exiting.

The Army is a funny place. Even though you are the same rank and in the same mess, there is an unwritten rule that, if you had the chance, you would laugh at and harass the other guy. So, as each group exited the "sugar shack" as the officers called it, the other groups would laugh hysterically as said group cried and snotted its way into the oxygen. Uncle Sam has a fairly twisted sense of humor.

CHAPTER 20

My civilian life continued on cruise control as I stumbled aimlessly through life with no apparent purpose. I now worked downtown for the state government and took my rightful place in the daily grinder. I worked 7a.m. to 4p.m. at my day job and 5p.m. to 9p.m. at my night time retail job. One TV show and one TV dinner later, I was ready for bed. This worked out pretty well as it didn't give me time during the week to think about Sarah and feel sorry for myself. Weekends, however, were brutal in that regard, so I continued my running to keep myself occupied.

My next competition was a race at the local rec center which drew a much smaller group of runners. I felt like a grizzled veteran as I had an entire 5 mile race under my belt. I lined up just behind the front line and waited for the starting gun. We started together and ran together for the first 1.5 miles. At that point, my mistake became very obvious. The people who were in the front of the starting line were good runners and could maintain a good pace for the entire five miles. Me, not so much. As I reached the two mile mark, I was sucking wind – bad. At the halfway point, I went into what is commonly known as the "survival shuffle". I shuffled, choked, and puked my way to the finish, having learned a lesson that I would remember forever – start slower than you expect to finish. I was ready to head to the car with my tail between my legs when I noticed that they had put up the results board. My time had been just over 40 minutes, well faster than my time in the first 5 miler. I confidently strutted back to my car, newly encouraged.

Having survived the rec center race, I returned to my mundane existence in which I looked forward to the workweek and dreaded the weekends. I was pretty fucked up, and allowed myself to wallow in a shitload of self-pity. However, the Good Lord was having none of it and sent me a message which went like "OK, asshole, pity party is way the fuck over (He didn't use those exact words). I'm sending you a sign that you will remember for the rest of your life. You're welcome".

The sign was a swift kick in the nuts which screamed "I am such an ungrateful prick." It came as I was leaving work and passing by a bus stop. I noticed that one of the people waiting for the bus was hunched over and had a deformed back. He was obviously a special needs case. As I waited to cross the street, he said "how are you doing? How was your day?" The enormity of the situation hit me like a brick to the face. Here was an individual whose life could be optimistically characterized as "bleak" asking me how I was doing. His smile was deafening. I managed to spit out "OK, how about you?" He said that he needed to hustle getting back to the special needs home where he lived because it was his night to cook. We exchanged "take cares" and went our separate ways. "Good one, Lord", I muttered to myself as I walked away, "next time just have a bus run over me".

CHAPTER 21

One thing that made one weekend a month less boring was Guard meetings. On this particular one, we went out to the boonies to set up the radios that were in the deuce and a halfs. The trucks were set up back to back with the tailgates down. This left a space of about two feet between the tailgates. It was an easy jump between trucks if you had full faculties. Aye, there's the rub. If, however, you had been partaking of the wildwood flower (as Jim Stafford called it), all bets were off. It just so happened that a couple of the boys were doing just that. To make things a little more complicated, this exercise was an overnighter. As the sun set over the Rockies and the skies darkened, the jump from one tailgate to the other became somewhat more complicated. As Roger Brown, who was now baked enough to make a French chef proud, made his way across the two foot abyss, his coordination and his spatial judgement failed him. All but his head and arms disappeared as he plummeted into the void. Each arm was propped onto a different tailgate. As the rest of us hurried to rush his broken body to the hospital, he muttered "Wow man, bummer! Can somebody give me a lift out of here?" He was definitely OK, but his armpits were going to be mega sore tomorrow.

This concluded the opening act of the evening, but the main event was still to come. To the side of each tailgate, a ground stake had been driven which served as a release for the voltage that the generators produced. As the night wore on and became pitch black, most of us opted to stay inside our respective vans, as venturing outside and onto a tailgate could certainly result in a repetition of the Brown fiasco. What we didn't figure on, however, was the call of nature. As specialist Anderson answered said call, he stood on one of the tailgates and let fly. Unfortunately for him, he peed on one of the ground stakes. The scream was not human and was probably heard in downtown Denver. He was knocked backwards and had to stop his pee stream, but the damage was done. Blue balls is never a fun time, but Anderson's balls were something else again, being a quite attractive combination of black, green and blue. Unlike Brown's fiasco, Anderson needed immediate medical attention. As the ambulance pulled away, we all wished him well and hoped that he would be attended to by a sweet nurse, who would put his rocks on ice.

CHAPTER 22

Sometimes, it's easy to count your blessings, especially when you haven't traumatized your armpits or electrified your johnson. Having avoided those two pitfalls, I went back to my work schedule. I also went about my running schedule, but made it a point to increase my mileage and to throw in a long run on weekends that didn't involve a guard meeting. Apparently, I wasn't the only person in the guard who ran. I found this out by reading race results in the newspaper. There was an annual event which entailed a 14.2 mile cruise to the top of Mount Evans, one of Colorado's 14ers. Names of all finishers were listed in the Sports section of the Rocky Mountain News. Sure enough, Ed Rupert's name was listed big as life. There are days when you wander around aimlessly looking for any type of motivation, and others when a particular object, item, or fact motivates you for years. Thus began my quest to conquer Mt. Evans.

Ed Rupert was a good guy. I had nothing against him. I did, however, feel a compulsion to conquer the mountain. The race started at 10,400 feet above sea level and ended at a cool 14,264 feet. The mountain was visible from almost anywhere in the city. This motivated me further. As I ran, I could look to the west and imagine the mountain laughing at me and saying "bring it, pussy! You don't have the stones!" Ergo, motivation wasn't a problem. The problems were twofold: hills and altitude. My usual course had a long, meandering hill which would do nicely. As far as the altitude went, there was no way I would travel to the mountains and back to get in a training run. First of all, I was already at 5,280 feet above sea level. Secondly, I figured I would go with the "get in, get done, get out" method. Visiting football teams would either employ my method or would try to "acclimate" by spending up to a week at altitude. I figured this gave the altitude the opportunity to really wear down and discourage someone. There was no way in my mind that someone could "acclimate" to the altitude without spending a minimum of 6 months.

I mixed 10 mile weekend runs in with my regular routine of 7 mile lunchtime runs at work. All the while, I could look west, see the mountain, and hear laughter. Every run was accompanied by a nagging thought that maybe I wasn't doing enough.

Finally, it arrived – race day. I had entered and gotten the T-shirt. Now, all I needed to do was complete the race. I always adhered to a couple of rules: If you don't finish the race, you don't wear the shirt, and you never wear the shirt for the race to the race.

I had picked up a few other tips during my running adventures: When you are running a marathon or comparable race, getting sleep the night before isn't a big factor. Getting sleep the night before the night before is the one that counts.

Having done everything I could think of to prepare, I made my way up I-70 to the Mt. Evans exit.

CHAPTER 23

Finding a parking space and exiting my car, I came to realize one of my runner fears. The other runners were mostly sleek, antelope looking beings that I had no business running with. I fed myself as much motivation talk as I could and then it was time to line up. As we lined up, I remembered when my folks took me fishing at Summit Lake, which is about 2/3 up the mountain. It was a cloudy, dreary day in Denver, but we decided to take a ride anyway. When we got to Summit Lake, the sun was shining brightly and we were above the clouds. I never forgot that trip.

As the runners lined up and got the starting gun, I concentrated on starting slow. You could see the leaders disappear into the trees. I was part of the last group. I had the other runners just where I wanted them. At about the four mile mark, we hit timberline. Above timberline, no vegetation could grow and the trees became twisted, bare, sticks. This would become a psychological challenge for me. My body was yelling "ignore that!" but my mind was saying "Holy Shit! If there isn't enough oxygen up here to sustain tree life, what in the Barney Fife fuck are we doing up here? That argument went on until we were uncomfortably above the four mile dead tree zone.

I employed one of my tricks to use on hill runs – shorten your stride and get your arms involved in your momentum. I had practiced this technique on the hills at home and found it to help. Soon, I established a rhythm and began passing people. Next we hit Summit Lake which had spectators, one of which had not acclimated to the altitude and had to leave via flight for life.

I had promised myself that if I made it to Summit Lake, there was no way I would not finish the race. However, the mountain had a final trick up its sleeve. Above Summit Lake there was a series of never ending switchbacks. When you completed one, another took its place – and another, and another. You could hear the commotion at the finish line, but the switchbacks never stopped coming – until the magic moment that they did. Never had I seen a more inviting finish line. As I crossed, a female volunteer helped me stumble along and told me how crazy I was for doing this. I thanked her and made my way as best I could to where the other runners were. My legs were apparently not finished running as they kept on moving at my running pace. That was weird. I made my way to the nearest rock and sat down. And wept.

THE END

AD MAJOREM DEI GLORIAM